Siesta

BY **Ginger Foglesong Guy**

PICTURES BY **René King Moreno**

Greenwillow Books, *An Imprint of* HarperCollins*Publishers*

Ven, osito.
Come, little bear.

¿Qué necesitamos? What do we need?

Mi mochila azul. **My** blue **backpack.**

¿Algo más?
Anything else?

Mi chaqueta roja.

My red jacket.

¿Algo más? Anything else?

Mi flauta verde. My green flute.

¿Algo más? Anything else?

Mi libro amarillo. My yellow book.

¿Algo más? Anything else?

Mi linterna negra. My black flashlight.

¿Algo más?
Anything else?

Mi reloj blanco. My white clock.

¿Algo más?
Anything else?

¡Sí! Algo azul, rojo, verde, amarillo, negro, y blanco.
Yes! Something blue, red, green, yellow, black, and white.

Mi manta.
My blanket.

¿Algo más?
Anything else?

No, está bien.
No, this is just right.

Carpa.

Tent.

Canción.

Song.

Descansa, descansa, osito, mi amigo.
Descansa, descansa, to sleep, a dormir.

Lie still and rest, little bear, my friend.
Lie still and rest, to sleep, a dormir.

Nap.

Siesta.

For Bob Smalldridge, my second father—G. F. G.

For Olivia—R. K. M.

Siesta. Text copyright © 2005 by Ginger Foglesong Guy. Illustrations copyright © 2005 by René King Moreno. All rights reserved.
Manufactured in China. www.harperchildrens.com
Rayo is an imprint of HarperCollins Publishers.

Pastels, watercolors, and pencils were used to prepare the full-color art. The text type is BerlinSans-Roma.

Library of Congress Cataloging-in-Publication Data
Guy, Ginger Foglesong. Siesta / by Ginger Foglesong Guy ; pictures by René King Moreno. p. cm. "Greenwillow Books."
Summary: A brother and sister and their teddy bear go through the house gathering items they will need for their siesta in the back yard.
ISBN 0-06-056061-4 (trade). ISBN 0-06-056063-0 (lib. bdg.). [1. Naps (Sleep)—Fiction. 2. Brothers and sisters—Fiction. 3. Teddy bears—
Fiction. 4. Spanish language materials—Bilingual.] I. Moreno, René King, ill. II. Title. PZ73.G842 2005 [E]—dc22 2004042464

First Edition 10 9 8 7 6 5 4 3 2 1
 Greenwillow Books